Evilution

I CONROY

DEDICATION

For my parents who instilled in me a love of books at an early age. They encouraged independent thinking, created an atmosphere of love and learning and encouraged me to dream big and follow my dreams.

For my family who supported me in this endeavor. For my children whom I love so very much.

For every child who dares to dream, wonder, question and think outside the box. Follow your dreams and never allow anyone to tell you can't achieve them.

ACKNOWLEDGMENTS

Help with review and publishing so graciously provided by my daughters.

For my Lord and Savior Jesus Christ who gave me words and inspiration to tell this story.

Chapter 1

"Don't worry, honey, you'll have fun this summer. Perhaps you will make some new friends back East. Why not just look at this as an adventure?" Twelve year old Justi did love the idea of an adventure; still this was not what she had in mind for summer vacation. Dad had just been deployed for the third time, this time to Afghanistan and after Mom lost her job, it was quickly decided the family would put their furniture in storage and go east to the area where Dad grew up, for the summer. There they could spend the summer rent-free and the kids could get to know the extended family they had not seen in many years. In California, Mom had worked part time and cared for her mother, who was sick for many years. Their grandmother passed recently and now their mother did not have anything to keep her in California. This trip would be a much needed rest for Mom.

As they drove along, nearing their destination in Kentucky, Justi couldn't even remember visiting, although Mom and Dad both assured her she had last visited when she was about 4 years old.

"Where are we going to stay?" Justi asked her Mom. "Well, honey, her mother answered, we're going to live in your dad's grandmother's house this summer. That's your great-grandmother. They call her Granny O. The old house is not in great shape, but the price is right. No one lives there anymore. Great grandmother lives with her daughter now because she's old and in poor health. The house was too much for her, so it's been sitting empty for some time. It's not a large house, but will more than meet our needs. I haven't seen it for years, but when daddy was a little boy, he loved to visit his grandmother there. He said she was a great story-teller and he loved to sit and listen to her stories for hours on end. He enjoyed hearing about how she grew up and the adventures she had as a young girl. I hear she was quite a different little girl. She loved fishing and being outdoors, but was a bit of a loner as well, preferring her books to most people." "Gosh, said

Justi, I don't remember Dad talking about his family much."
"That's because most of the time that you remember, your Dad
was deployed. When he was home, there was just so much to do,
and so little time," Mom answered.

When the car pulled up in front of the white frame house, Justi
nearly gasped. Were they really going to live in *this* house? It
looked so old and run down. This was worse than she had
expected. It had been a long drive and she and Parker reluctantly
climbed out of the car and headed toward the front door. Mom
found the key that was hidden just above the ledge and unlocked
the door. They stepped inside and, Justi thought, back in time. It
was obvious that someone had tidied up. There was no dust, but
the house had a musty smell. There was a living room with some
old, but clean furniture and a dining room with a round oak table
and 6 sturdy, well-worn chairs. The kitchen was small and
outdated. The counter tops were yellow Formica with a stainless
steel edge, right out of the 1950s. This was nothing like the house
they had spent their lives in back home in California. There were
three small bedrooms on the first floor and one large bathroom. Off
of the living room, there was a small room, almost an alcove - that
had tall bookshelves, with lots of dusty, old books. Justi thought to
herself," this is how people lived before computers and e-books.
How boring! Still, she felt certain warmth come over her as she
remembered Dad and was reminded that she was standing in a
place that he loved. Perhaps, that would help her get through this
ordeal. She was a girl who loved an adventure. In fact, she wasn't
like most other girls her age. She loved to read, using her Kindle,
of course, and she loved to investigate. Justi had always been
independent and responsible beyond her years. She was a good
student, especially strong in math and science and she was a good
athlete. Because of her natural curious nature she often thought
perhaps one day, she'd be a detective. She loved a good mystery.
She adjusted her dark pony tail and headed toward the kitchen to
explore her new surroundings.

There was food in the kitchen along with a welcome note left by
Dad's aunt Gert. Fried chicken, potato salad and baked beans.
There were homemade yeast rolls pecan pie.   Not exactly

California cuisine, but it would have to do. After all, they were hungry and tired. It turned out to be pretty good, not something Mom would cook, but also not so bad. In fact, it was pretty good.

Over the next few days, Justi and her brother, Parker, who was 9, explored the neighborhood and met a few kids who were near their ages. One afternoon, while they were out playing, the sky darkened, and the wind started to blow and thunder rumbled overhead. The kids headed home, making it inside just before the rain started. It was clear that they had to spend the rest of the afternoon inside. Justi, who had simply tolerated this disgusting, old house so far, decided this might be a good time to explore. Maybe there was something that could hold her interest. Mom had not turned on the cable or internet, probably on purpose, and Justi was tired of her hand-held games after three days of them during the car ride last week.

This house was large by California standards, with a nice porch and a large yard, even though it was in town. She started with the dusty books, but quickly lost interest. She poked around in the cabinets and the closets and found they were mostly empty. She opened the last closet, and it was not a closet at all! Behind that door was a small staircase. It was dark and dusty, and smelled like those old books. She quickly found the light switch and started up the stairs. They creaked and groaned and she left footprints in the dust as she slowly made her way up. Once at the top of the stairs, she was surprised to see a large room with a window in one end. There were boxes stacked all around the walls, but the main floor was uncluttered. It had a chair and desk and a two other chairs. There was a small bookshelf near the desk. The window was so dirty that it was hard to see outside. The dark sky and rain sure didn't help.

Justi was a curious girl. She loved a mystery and she loved to explore. This attic looked like it might contain a mystery. She poked around in boxes and found the typical things that people store in their attics – old Christmas decorations, clothes, kitchen items and some old children's toys and books. There were some pictures which might contain clues. She took note of this box for further investigation later.

For some unexplained reason, she was drawn to the small desk that was positioned near the window. She sat down and began to pretend that she was a girl who lived long ago, sitting in the attic on a rainy day. What would a girl from those days do? Write perhaps or read. Maybe listen to the radio. They did have radio back then, didn't they? She wondered how those poor kids ever managed to live without cell phones, video games, e-readers and oh, yes, television. She was very glad to be a modern girl.

She started to open drawers in the desk and found a few pencils, an old eraser that had gotten hard over the years and she noted, was useless. In the back of the top drawer, she noticed a yellowed scrap of paper caught between the top and back of the drawer. She tugged on it and a corner ripped off. Ooops! She worked the drawer up and down and finally, the paper was freed. It contained three curious words, "I like monk …" The rest of the paper was long gone. Justi thought that was an odd thing to find in a desk drawer, in an attic in Kentucky and wondered who sat at this desk long ago and wrote those words. What was the rest of that phrase? Justi struggled to come up with possible words: monkeys, monkfish, monks, she could not think of another word. Justi decided it must be either monkeys or monks. Justi enjoyed the monkeys at the zoo so perhaps the writer was also a fan of monkeys? Either way, it was a strange message. Perhaps this was a mystery that needed to be solved.

When her mother returned from the grocery store, Justi ran to help unload the car and tell Mom what she had discovered in the attic. "Mom, she pleaded, can I use the attic to get away from Parker while we're here? You know I like a quiet place where I can read." Mom replied that perhaps they could clean up a bit and Justi could use the attic, so long as she didn't disturb anything that was stored there. After dinner, with the rain still pouring down outside, Justi returned to the attic to explore some more. She went back to the desk. There was something odd she needed to check out. The desk had three drawers on each side. However, she noticed that one of the drawers was not as deep as the others. This made her wonder if it had a hidden compartment. A hidden compartment might contain a mystery. She'd read stories of desks with secret drawers and big old houses with walls that moved to reveal hidden rooms. If there was a secret drawer, it might be a perfect place to store things, away from Parker's prying eyes.

Justi slid open the drawer on the left side and pushed, pulled and tugged, but nothing happened. Oh well, it was a fun thought. Maybe this was just a weird, old desk. As she tried to close the drawer, it stuck and wouldn't slide. Dad would say that was from the humidity, and they certainly had humidity today. As she worked the drawer forward and backward, her fingers touched something that was like a small lever. She pushed on it hard and it moved just a little. A few more tugs and a secret compartment was revealed. To her disappointment, there was only a stack of old, yellowed paper in the drawer. She thumbed through it, to confirm it was all blank. That's when she noticed a small brown book tucked into the back corner. This house was full of old books, but why hide one? She lifted it out and quickly realized this was not a book. It was a journal – someone's private journal. Without hesitation or thought about the privacy of the writer, the girl detective began to read.

When Mom called for dinner, Justi slid the journal in her pack and headed downstairs. During dinner Mom said that over the next few weeks they would meet more of Dad's family. Plans were not complete yet, but she wanted to be sure they got to visit with dad's relatives they hadn't seen since they were young. In fact, neither Justi nor Parker remembered any of the people Mom mentioned. Parker immediately began to complain that he didn't want to meet a bunch of old, boring people who would probably say things like, "oh my, how you've grown!," pinch his cheeks and exclaim he was cute and other equally stupid things that adults say to kids when they don't know anything else to say. Mom told Parker that attitude would not do and he needed to mind his manners. He just sighed and said, "Yes Ma'am." For Justi, the wheels had started to turn and she was beginning to formulate a plan. She was actually looking forward to meeting Dad's relatives.

That night, when she went to bed, Justi reached into her pack and pulled out the journal. Like any good detective, there were items she could not be without. She had a pen light that was not much bigger than an ink pen, small but bright, it easily fit in her pocket. She always had paper and a pen or pencil, and a magnifying glass, and a small pair of binoculars, the kind that collapse into a small pouch. Since she had a nice, new, smartphone she often took notes on it, using an app or the voice recorder. In fact, the smart phone was a great tool for a detective. It had a flashlight feature and a camera for stills or video. Those gumshoes in the 1940s movies she loved to watch with Dad would never have imagined technology like this! Under the covers, she took out her smart phone and used the flashlight to return to reading the journal. She read almost half of it before she started to nod off.

Chapter 2

Justi woke early the next morning, just as the light started to stream in her window. She immediately remembered the journal and while she wanted to finish reading, she did not want anyone to discover this little treasure. She needed to do some detective work first. She slid the journal into her pack, got dressed and headed into the kitchen. Mom wasn't up yet, and she knew Parker was still asleep as well, so she ate some cereal and then grabbed her pack and very quietly, tiptoed up the creaky old stairs to the attic. Here, she could continue to read the journal without being discovered. It was all hand written, and it seemed to span several years. By the time she smelled coffee brewing and heard Mom call out to her, it was nearly 7:30 and Justi was almost finished with her reading. As she read, she made notes of important facts like dates and events. Her plan was starting to come together. There was just one problem – this journal was not what she expected and it was a little bit scary. She was not sure if it was a journal and represented a true story or the product of someone's imagination. At any rate, it was interesting.

When Mom called a second time, Justi headed downstairs. There were some chores to do and then she could return to her reading. She joined Mom in the kitchen for bagels and fresh fruit. "Mom, Justi said, tell me about Dad's family – the ones you said we'll meet next week." "Well, let's see said Mom, there is Aunt Gert who is your Dad's aunt, and Uncle Jim, the one with the farm, then there is Jim's wife Kate and their daughter Meg…Mom paused, the O'Connor clan is quite large. I guess long ago many families were large with 8, 10 or even 15 kids. There are a lot of them and some have nicknames. It is hard to keep their nicknames and their real names straight. For example, there is Toot who is really Fiona, Agnes is Sister, Brud I think, is really named Brian, Butch is Barry, Bitsy is Elizabeth, Bessie is Bridget and on my, I can't remember the rest right now. Granny O lives with Bitsy, one of her daughters. Granny O, Brud, Butch and Bessie, Billi and Toot are siblings and are some of the ones who grew up in this house. As I said, it was a big family, but many of them have already passed on." "Wow!" said Justi, "that is confusing. What else can you tell me?" Mom thought for a minute then said, "I think the O'Connors, like many Irish folks, love to talk and they love to tell stories. They are a fun-loving bunch and a close family. They are silly and funny and as I remember, they love music. Being around Dad's clan is rarely boring. I think you're going to enjoy meeting them."

After making her bed, sweeping the front porch and helping with the dishes, Justi was free to return to her attic hideaway and her reading. She sat down at the desk and carefully took the small, leather volume out of her pack. She looked in the front and the back for the name of the owner, but once again, found nothing. She continued to read and just when she reached an important part of the story, she heard Parker bounding up the attic stairs. She quickly slid the book into the top desk drawer and turned to face her brother. He was hot and sweaty, obviously, he'd been outside playing. He was panting as he asked her to join in a baseball game with some of the neighborhood kids. He explained that they were one short and could really use another kid fast. Justi hesitated, but soon relented and hurried downstairs to grab her shoes and baseball glove. She wanted to finish her reading, but it was also a little bit scary. She just read a part about ghosts. There is nothing like a bright, sunny morning to take your mind off of something that's a little spooky, she thought.

Justi and Parker enjoyed the game and getting to know some of the neighborhood kids. The yards here were much bigger than in California, even though this house was in the city. The kids played ball in an empty lot down the street so no one put a baseball through the window of a house or nearby car. It was a good game and after the game, Parker and Justi joined some of the other kids for lemonade in the backyard of Big Joe, one of the neighborhood kids. Big Joe was a nice kid, tall with dark, curly hair and brown eyes. He looked more like a football player than a baseball player and Justi was surprised to learn he was only 11. It turned out that Big Joe was very athletic and he was a good hitter. When he stepped to the plate, both the infield and the outfielder players started moving back. The kids talked about their respective schools and Justi and Parker explained what life was like in California to the other kids. They hurried towards home when the sky started to darken and Big Joe predicted another summer thunderstorm was coming soon.

Back at the house, they filled Mom in on the neighborhood kids and the game over a late lunch. Parker headed for the living room to play his video games and Justi grabbed her pack and headed up the attic stairs to finish her reading. She settled in at the desk and began to read just as the storm started to hit. The wind was bending the tree branches and the sky was almost as dark as night. The wind howled outside the window and the motion of the trees against the dark sky made the attic feel more than a little spooky. This really isn't a good time to be reading about ghosts, thought Justi, but being a detective, she was naturally curious, so she continued despite the storm.

Justi was both surprised and a little confused about what she read. However, by now, the plan was well-formed in her mind. She just needed more detail. First, a list of "suspects." She pulled up the notes app on her phone. After talking to Mom, Justi had entered all of the names she could remember that Mom listed. She added to her previous entry:

Suspects

All women in this family over the age of 75, dead or alive.

Granny O

Bessie

Billi

Toot

Unknown others like aunts or cousins

Facts

Earliest date in journal - 1936

All entries written by same person (high probability)

Person who wrote this journal likes to read

Person who wrote this journal was female

Person who wrote this journal was curious

Person who wrote this journal was probably a child or young adult

Person who wrote this journal was interested in ghosts

Justi reviewed her list. A good detective must always cast her net wide when considering suspects. She must deal in facts. She must review her assumptions and make corrections along the way. She must keep an open mind. She must always record any new facts or events immediately in order to retain as much information as possible. Since the facts reveal that the writer is female, the men, assuming they are men, can be crossed off the list.

She made more notes about how she would approach this task. She would not reveal that she'd found the journal, but rather attempt to learn the identity of the writer through casual conversation. Of course, all male relatives are immediately eliminated. Justi imagined the conversation going something like this:

Female Relative: Justi, how old are you now?

Justi: 12

Relative: what grade are you in?

Justi: going to be in 7th in the fall

Relative: other questions about school, like favorite subject, etc.

Justi: answers concluding with, I like books and I like to read, do you?

Relative: yes or no

Justi: if yes, continue the questioning of the suspect. If no, find a way to end the conversation and move on.

Justi: If yes, discuss authors and raise the authors specially mentioned in the journal.

If the answers are affirmative, continue with this suspect. If not, move on to the next suspect after taking good notes.

Justi: continue the questioning/discussions and then, at the appropriate moment, throw the curve ball. Make the statement that only the author of the journal will understand and use observation skills to watch the face.

Justi knew the face was always the best way to gauge whether someone is being truthful. She would throw her curve ball (monks) to the elderly relative and watch. If she was indeed speaking with the author of the journal, the author would have a "tell." A tell is a non-verbal clue like a gesture, fidget, motion, expression or movement that a person exhibits when they are concealing the truth or being deceptive. Poker players try to determine the tell of the other players so they know when the player is bluffing. Justi learned about tells by listening to Dad and his poker buddies talk. Because Justi was quiet and would sit in a big chair and read, adults often forgot she was around. Detectives watch for the classic signs of a tell when questioning suspects or witnesses. Some signs are touching the face or hands, crossing the arms and not directly answering the question. For example, answering the question with a question, stalling in some way or even leaning back. If she saw a tell or a facial expression that would be a good indication she had her woman. Justi would continue with her plan. She would follow up with her second curve ball, which was also a prominent part of this journal, and watch carefully.

Her plan was coming together. Justi hoped that the author was still alive and willing to talk. She had one more decision to make. Should she take the journal with her or leave it at home locked safely in the secret compartment in the desk? Justi was well aware that the journal did not belong to her. After reading it, she simply felt compelled to know more. It was about ghosts but it was not the usual ghost story. It appeared to be written by a child or adolescent. Was it a story, the figment of an over-active imagination or could it be true? Justi felt she needed to know the answer to that question before she returned to California in a few weeks. For now, she returned the journal to its secret compartment, turned the desk lamp off, grabbed her pack and headed downstairs.

Chapter 3

Finally, the day of the family picnic arrived and Justi could hardly wait. This picnic was an annual event, a tradition with Dad's family, at least the ones who lived nearby. Mom said some of the relatives who lived a little further were coming as well since it was a rare occasion for Mom, Justi and Parker to be back East and able to attend. They were up early and packed the car with the items Mom felt they should bring a cooler with lots of bottled water, some folding chairs, a large fruit salad and of course enough sunscreen to cover at least one battalion of the army. Sunscreen was almost a religion with Mom. She never left home without it.

Last night Justi made the decision to leave the journal tucked safely away in the attic desk. She felt responsible for its safety and it was old and should be handled with care. She had her pack as always because it contained important tools and some items to keep her entertained if this picnic was just too boring to tolerate.

They were headed out into the country to the farm of Uncle Jim and Aunt Kate. It was over 50 acres in the rolling hills about 45 minutes outside of town. Mom said it was a working farm, and that Jim and Kate grew corn, green beans, tomatoes and other summer crops including many different fruits and vegetables. Jim sold to local grocery stores and directly at the local farmer's market.

Mom told them that Jim and Kate built a large shelter on the property with picnic tables, restrooms, and charcoal grills nearby. They built it a few years back for family gatherings and for their farm business. It was a dual purpose shelter, used for parties and other events. Because it was hard to make a living in farming these days, Jim and Kate had diversified. They hosted school and church groups for tours of the farm. They promoted events for families to come pick their own vegetables and offered hay rides in the fall that included a ride around the farm on the hay wagon pulled by a tractor and a bon fire for roasting weenies and marshmallows and they served hot chocolate after the ride.

Mom continued that there should be a lot of their cousins at the farm and she hoped they would make friends quickly and have a great day. They would get to explore the farm and have some new experiences. Justi was thinking only of the older relatives and could not focus on playing kids' games. She had her notes in her phone and being prepared for any disaster that might come along, she always had a backup plan, so she had a hard copy as well. She'd gone over many possible scenarios in her mind and she hoped that by the end of the day, she would have solved the mystery of the author. But that was just the first step. She wanted to find a way to engage the author so she could ask questions about the journal. While reading, there were times she'd become confused and needed clarification. Justi found herself hoping against hope that the author was still living. What if the author was dead? Perhaps this mystery would never be solved. The girl detective did not know it, but her day was going to be much more interesting than she had ever imagined.

They drove along with Mom following the directions on the GPS and Justi checking them with the printed directions provided by Aunt Gert. Mom explained that sometimes a GPS is not accurate when you get too far off of the main roads. She didn't want to get lost and drive into a corn field or do something else equally stupid like you sometimes heard happened to people who relied too heavily on the GPS and not enough on common sense.

As they continued on their trip, they drove further from the city or what Parker like to call civilization, and deeper into the country. Cool air drifted out of the hollows. Mom explained these were the deep valleys between the hills which often contained a creek. Locals referred to them as hollers. The air was crisp and clean and the kids rolled the windows down to take in the sweet smell of honeysuckle growing wild by the roadside.

The road alternated between being shady and sunny depending on whether they were passing hilly land or flat farmland. They passed farms with cattle and horses grazing in pastures and large cornfields that went on for as far as the eye could see. The houses were much further apart now and a small creek ran along one side of the road. It was quiet here, with only the occasional sound of a mower or tractor to interrupt the sounds of nature. Justi had to admit she felt peaceful here. Parker was only worried about whether they might get lost and whether there was electricity, cell phone towers and internet service this far away from the city. Mom assured him he had no reason to worry.

Chapter 4

The GPS was off now, deemed useless after it instructed Mom to "turn right in 500 feet" which would have resulted in their car turning into the neatly mowed yard of a farm house. When it insisted on repeating, "make a U turn whenever possible" over and over, Mom shut it off. Justi was the navigator now and it appeared they were getting close to the final turn on Aunt Gert's directions. They all watched closely for the narrow road beside a mailbox on the right side that Aunt Gert described as looking more like a driveway than a road. They spotted the number, 324 on the mailbox and Mom made the turn. The road was too narrow for more than one car to pass at a time. Mom spotted the driveway and turned right. The drive was wide and lined with trees. It led up to a large, white clapboard house with a wrap-around porch and tall columns on the front. The house sat in the shade of two very large oak trees. Chairs with large, colorful cushions lined the porch. Justi thought the house looked like it was inviting you to come up and sit down for a glass of iced tea and a chat. Mom followed the driveway and as she came closer to the house a young boy came running out and waved and yelled to them to drive the car around behind the barn and park there.

Mom parked and the kids quickly exited the car. Mom called to them to help with the cooler. After unloading, Parker and Justi started toward a small group of kids passing a Frisbee in the field. Mom gave them a quick look that sent a message loud and clear: Where are your manners? Quickly, the two came back to say hello and meet the relatives that were sitting under the shelter. Mom walked up to a thin man, probably a few years older than Dad, wearing khaki pants, suspenders and a plaid shirt. His skin was tan, and his hands calloused. "Hello, he exclaimed with a warm smile. I'm Jim. Do you remember me, Julie?" "Yes, of course I do, Mom replied. It's good to see you, Jim, it's been too long, she said, giving him a hug. This is Parker and Justi. Kids, this is your Dad's older brother, your Uncle Jim." "Welcome to our farm, Jim said. Kate is around here somewhere. We're so glad you are here!" The kids shook hands with Uncle Jim and said nice to meet you. They said hello to Aunt Gert and met Bitsy and Sister. Then they looked at Mom who nodded her approval allowing them to head out into the field to play. She told them not to go too far. Julie spent the next half hour chatting with Danny's relatives and catching up on family news.

After playing Frisbee and meeting some of her cousins, Justi returned to the shelter for some water and to check out the relatives. Bitsy and Sister were not old enough to be the author. Justi pulled out her phone and took a quick look at her notes to review the suspect's names. Uncle Jim had a large grill fired up and was starting to cook hamburgers and hot dogs. The smell of food reminded Justi that she was hungry. She wandered around the long picnic tables eyeing the food. One end of the table had pasta salad, potato salad, tossed salad, watermelon, cucumber salad, macaroni salad, fruit salad, sliced tomatoes, trays of fresh vegetables and dips and a variety of breads. Another table contained a variety of pies, cakes, cookies and sweet treats. Justi thought to herself, the O'Connor clan sure knows how to throw a party! As she was staring at a plate of large, soft ginger cookies with thick white icing, she felt someone beside her. She looked over to see a tall, thin woman, smartly dressed in a white tunic and navy slacks. She was a strikingly handsome woman with her white hair swept up off her neck, finger nails painted deep red and makeup perfectly done. "Hello, the woman said, I'm Fiona, but everyone calls me Aunt Toot." "Nice to meet you, I'm Justice Leigh, but everyone calls me Justi," she said extending her hand. Justi was surprised by how thin and bony the older woman's fingers were and by the strength of her grip. Toot continued, "I'm your great-grandmother's sister, or one of them anyway. You'll meet Bessie too, she's another sister, just a year older than Liza, both are considerably older than I," she said. "Oh, OK," Justi said trying desperately to come up with more conversation so she could start her questioning of this suspect. This is not going well, she thought. Toot continued her chatter, "So, I hear you're staying in our old home place while you're visiting. Tell me what you're doing to keep yourself busy this summer." Thinking quickly, Justi said, "We've met some kids in the neighborhood and played ball a few times and I've done some reading. I really enjoy reading, do you?" Oh, of course, I do child, when we were children reading was good entertainment. Of course, back then we didn't have television to distract us or computers, we just had radio. Kids these days have a variety of gadgets that we didn't have." "Do you like Socrates?" Justi asked keeping her eyes locked on Aunt Toot's face. "Yes, dear, I suppose I do" she said haltingly. Clearly Toot was confused by this rather odd question from a twelve year old girl, but she showed no interest in discussing Socrates. Justi tried again, saying "I find Herodotus interesting." She watched Aunt Toot's face closely. No reaction. "Yes...well...you must be studying Herodotus in school – that's good." said Aunt Toot. Justi followed with, I've been reading about ghosts. Do you like to read about ghosts?" Again, Justi watched closely as she said these words. Aunt Toot's face looked a little confused, "no, honey, I don't really like to read about ghosts." I'm striking out, Justi thought to herself. I'll try one last topic on her. "I'm interested in monks," Justi said with a grin. She watched Aunt Toot's face closely. Poor Aunt Toot looked a little puzzled. After a minute of silence, she said, "That is an odd interest for a young lady, but each to her own." Justi decided that Aunt Toot could not be the author. She failed the test. At no time did she take any of the bait. It was time to find a way out of this conversation and move on to the next suspect. Justi looked at Aunt Toot, then said, "Excuse me, I need to check in with my Mom. It has been nice chatting with you." With that she was off. Justi jogged away from Aunt Toot but stopped just around the corner where she couldn't be seen and pulled out her phone. She made some quick notes beside Aunt Toot's name about her reactions to Socrates, Herodotus, ghosts and monks. Then, she went to find her next suspect. She found Mom and told her she'd met Aunt Toot and had a nice conversation. She and Mom walked over toward the grill and talked with Uncle Jim. He said the burgers would be done soon and told Justi to let the other kids know they would eat in a few minutes. Justi ran off to tell the kids and to think about her conversation with Aunt Toot. There was no reaction to her curve ball – monks by Aunt Toot. Perhaps she was the author, but she just didn't catch the hints Justi was dropping. Or maybe the hints weren't good enough. Maybe she should have used more clues from the journal. Maybe, Aunt Toot was too old to remember. The possibilities were a little troubling. Justi told herself the plan was good and it would work if she found the real author, provided she was still alive.

Justi ran over to let the kids know it was time to eat and then she walked back to the shelter with them. The smell of food filled the air and she realized that she was very hungry. She got a paper plate and stood in the burger line. After choosing small amounts of many different dishes, Justi chose a place at the picnic table near Parker and several of their cousins. Some of the older relatives she had not yet met were at the other end of the table. They were chatting and laughing, telling stories about things they'd done as kids. After a few minutes, Justi figured out that one of the men was Butch and the other was Brud. They were telling about a time that they had been playing in the neighborhood with the some of their friends. Butch said, "There was a big snow on the ground and we were all sledding down the hill. We decided to find a bigger hill so we could go faster. There was a creek at the bottom of the bigger hill and we decided to go down on our sleds and let this big pile of leaves at the bottom stop us so we didn't go in the creek. We thought that was a pretty good idea." Brud chimed in, "Except poor ol' Jack jumped on his sled and headed down the hill. He picked up speed and was hoopin' and hollerin' and about that time, he hit that pile of leaves and that sled stopped dead! Those leaves were frozen solid as a rock, something we hadn't considered." Butch laughed and picked up the story, "the sled stopped but Jack didn't. He went flyin' through the air and came down on the other side of that creek. Probably would have killed him if the snow hadn't been so deep." They both laughed and most of the others around the table laughed too, even though they had all heard that story before. Justi liked the way Butch and Brud told stories and thought to herself that if she didn't have some serious detective work to do, she would listen a while longer. She was starting to see what Mom meant about the O'Connor's being Irish story tellers.

As she listened to the story, Justi looked around the picnic shelter. She spotted several older women, among them she hoped to meet Billi, Bessie and Granny O. About that time, Mom waved to her from another picnic table. She picked up her plate and drink and passed by the trash can to deposit her trash. She went over to speak to Mom and see who she might meet next.

Mom was sitting with Aunt Kate and a few other cousins. Justi met Kate who had dark shoulder length hair and a warm smile. Justi, "this is Aunt Kate and her daughter Meg, your cousins Jill and Annie" Mom said. "Hi, it's nice to meet you. Thank you for having us." Just as she was wondering what to say next, Justi noticed two women walking arm in arm, talking and laughing as they headed toward the table. One was slightly taller than the other. They moved with ease. The taller one was dressed in white Capri pants a navy striped cotton shirt and navy flats. Her dark hair was cut short and peppered with gray. She wore small tortoise shell glasses. The shorter one wore beige Capri pants with a black and beige cotton top and beige espadrilles. She had curly dark hair that framed her face and had only a slight bit of gray. Her frameless glasses were almost invisible. Justi studied them and decided they were sisters. They looked a lot alike and there was something about the way they related to each other that told even a casual observer that they had a very close relationship. "Oh, here comes Bessie and Granny O exclaimed Meg. Justi, they are such a hoot! You're going to enjoy them so much! Prepare to be entertained." Justi looked at Meg, then looked back at the pair and thought they looked much younger than she had imagined. They did not appear to be typical little old ladies, and where was the "poor health" that caused Granny O to have to live with her daughter? She looked perfectly fine, in fact she looked quite spry. Justi began to wonder how she would question these suspects if they were inseparable. Up to this point, she had imagined one on one conversations with her suspects. Perhaps it was time to re-think her strategy. Granny O and Bessie almost danced up to the table. They were laughing and smiling, still arm in arm. Bessie said, "Oh, this must be Justi! My how you've grown, you were just a little thing last time you were here. Of course we see your pictures regularly, but there's nothing like seeing you in person." With that she reached out for a big hug. Just stood and hugged her realizing that Aunt Bessie was pretty strong for an old lady. Granny O followed with her hug and said, "We're so happy to see you all of you! Julie come here and give me a hug. Where is Parker? I want to see that young man. He looks so much like Danny in the pictures you sent." Julie replied, "Yes, I agree, he looks a lot like Danny. He'll be around when he's hungry again. I think he's off playing with his cousins. Thank you, Granny for the use of your house. The kids and I really appreciate your hospitality." Granny O smiled, "You're welcome to stay there as long as you like. You know I was perfectly fine living alone, but I got sick one time, was in the hospital, just as a precaution, and Bitsy panicked. Honestly, I think she was just lonely. I can still work circles around her." Justi was surprised by the comments and by the fact that Granny O was so lively. It was obvious she was independent and opinionated, both qualities Justi admired. Justi was expecting the stereotypical great grandmother with a cane and someone helping her out of her chair. Her own grandmother on her mother's side was in poor health so long that Justi never imagined that a great-grandmother could seem so young and lively. Justi's job might be harder than she originally imagined.

Butch stood up shouted and motioned to Granny O to come over to his table. She sighed and put a hand on her hip. "OK, Butch, just give me a minute. I'll come to you since I'm younger and in better shape than you, old man," she called with a laugh. Come on Julie, let's go see what that crazy brother of mine wants. Julie got up to go to Granny O and Bessie sat down. She looked at Justi and said," Tell me dear, are you enjoying your visit? Have you done anything fun since you've been here?" Mostly we've just played with kids in the neighborhood and I've been reading some. Do you like to read, she asked Bessie? "Oh, my yes, I love to read. When we were kids we read a lot because we didn't have TV. Mom and Dad would read and when they took us fishing, we would sit around the fire and tell stories until late at night." Now, thought Justi, we're getting somewhere. "I like Socrates and I find Herodotus interesting as well," she said watching Bessie's face closely. "The problem I see with Socrates is that we depend on his students, like Plato for our information. But, then if you've studied Socrates, you're aware of that. As for Herodotus, I find him quite entertaining. He recorded history, but some of his stories were somewhat fanciful." This is good thought Justi. Finally, some progress. Perhaps, Bessie is the author. As she listened, Justi plotted her next move. I'm also interested in reading about ghosts,

Justi stated with the cool demeanor of a scientist. Bessie was silent for a minute but she did not react. Her face looked a little puzzled. Slowly, she said, "Socrates, Herodotus and ghost stories…now that is quite a combination! I'm not terribly interested in ghosts mostly because I don't believe they exist. However, I will grant to you they make for good storytelling. Our family has been known to tell a ghost story or two, I think. What else interests you?" Justi was ready for this opening and without hesitation, she threw her curve ball. "I like monks." Bessie looked a little surprised, then said, "All right dear, but *why* do you like monks? Do you know any?" Not expecting this response, but knowing she needed to closely paraphrase the journal, Justi replied, "No, I don't know any monks personally, but I like Monks and I like Monasteries. Monks are to be admired. They pray, work and earn money with the sale of articles they produce." Justi delivered these lines with enthusiasm while she looked intently at Bessie, summoning all of her concentration to observe her suspect's face and body language. Bessie only looked confused. She was staring at Justi with a mixture of curiosity, confusion and surprise. Bessie was either not the author or she'd forgotten everything she wrote. At some point during their conversation, Meg had quietly slipped away and was chatting with some relatives at the other end of the shelter. Bessie smiled at Justi and said, "One thing is for sure, my dear - you are O'Connor through and through! We pride ourselves on being interesting, well-read and entertaining, and we all love a good conversation. You certainly inherited the O'Connor's gift of gab. I have enjoyed our visit. Right now, I'm thinking of eating some desert and having a nice cup of tea. Will you join me?" Oh, no thank you, Justi replied. I ate so much I'm afraid there is no room for desert. I enjoyed our conversation as well." With that, Justi made her exit and slipped away to make notes about Bessie in her phone.

Justi spent the next hour or two playing, exploring and waiting for an opportunity to talk to Granny O alone. She feared the day would end and she would not get her chance. Granny O and Bessie had gone back to the house shortly after Justi finished her conversation with Bessie. When Aunt Kate offered Julie a tour of their house, Justi decided to tag along. She followed Kate and Mom on the long path that led from the shelter back to the big house. The house was warm and inviting and the large porch reminded Justi of a picture right out of a magazine. The comfortable chairs that were blue and yellow with colorful print cushions and there were flowers everywhere. Justi noted that the ceiling of the porch was painted light blue. She had never see that before and made a quick mental note to ask about it. There was a dog, mostly brown in color but with a little black mixed in, sleeping on the front porch. He opened an eye and raised his head just a little as they approached, then went back to sleep. Justi loved animals so she asked Kate about him. His name is Gus, Kate told her. He's been with us a long time. Like most of our pets, he was a rescue. He's a good dog. You can pet him. He's as gentle as a lamb. That was all Justi needed to hear. She ran up to Gus and bent down to speak to him. He opened his eyes and then raised his head. Justi held out her hand so he could sniff and give her the signal that it was Ok to touch him. Gus sniffed her hand, gave it a short lick and then rolled onto his side, inviting her to pet him and rub his belly. Justi was thrilled by this and she petted him and talked to him like he was a person. They became friends instantly. Justi had always wanted a dog, but because they never knew where the army might send them, understood that it was not a good idea. We're going inside, Mom called to her. Justi started to walk away and Gus got up to follow. She walked onto the porch and Gus followed. As they were about to enter the house, Gus turned and walked around the to the side porch. Justi decided to follow him. As she turned the corner, she could see that Gus was trotting to greet Granny O, who was sitting in a rocking chair sipping her tea. "Hello, Gus, Granny O said with a smile. I see you've finished your nap." Just then, she spotted Justi trailing behind Gus. "And you've made a new friend, too I see. Hello, Justi. I see you've met Gus. He's such a good dog! "Yes, replied Justi. I love dogs, but we've never been able to have one. He is so sweet, I just instantly fell in love with him." Granny O smiled at her. "Come, sit down with me and Gus. Would you like a cup of tea?" No thank you, Justi said. But I will sit down with you and Gus." Gus quickly settled in between Justi and Granny O, carefully placing himself closer to Justi than to the rocking chair. Gus is a smart dog. He understands not to get too close to my rocker, Granny O pointed out. Have you had enough to eat, Justi? "I think I probably had too much, Justi exclaimed. Everything was so good! I just wanted to taste as much as possible." You like to try new foods? Yes, I guess I'm just naturally curious, Justi told her. I guess that is why I enjoy reading. As I was telling Aunt Bessie earlier, I like Socrates and Herodotus Justi stated while turning to look directly at Granny O. She thought she noticed one eyebrow raise just slightly, but she wasn't sure. Granny O smiled and asked if her interest was related to studying the ancient Greeks at school. No, Justi told her, just something I read recently. I do enjoy mysteries and sometimes I like ghost stories. No noticeable reaction, so Justi took a deep breath and waited. What kind of ghost stories do you enjoy? Justi thought then said, "Unusual ghost stories, I suppose are the best." She looked at Granny O as she imagined how she might deliver her curve ball. She waited to see if the conversation would take a different turn. "Well, said Granny O slowly, I suppose unusual is better than the same old thing, isn't it?" Justi nodded. She petted Gus almost absent mindedly as she waited to see what Granny O had to say next. Silence. Granny O sipped her tea and rocked, saying nothing at all. She looked at Justi intently. Finally, she spoke, "You look a little bit like I did when I was your age," she said to Justi. Justi smiled but waited for her to go on. I was a curious young woman as well. Tell me, what else interests you?" This was the opening Justi had waited for. She looked directly at Granny O and summoned the courage to deliver her curve ball. In her head, she could hear a baseball announcer saying, the windup, the pitch...Justi blinked the voice out of her head and said, "I like monks." Granny O's eyes got wide and she looked over her glasses at Justi, her dark eyes locked on Justi's face. Without blinking, Justi forced the words that were caught in her throat to come out, "and I like Monasteries." This time, Justi saw the surprise on Granny O's face, but there was also a look that might be anger. Justi felt a little bit afraid. She had, after all, read a private journal that she had no business reading. Granny O was silent but her gaze was intent. Justi did not dare look away. Granny O spoke first. "Interesting. Why do you like monks and monasteries?" Justi repeated the words she'd read in the journal. "Monks are to be admired. They pray, work and earn money with the sale of articles they produce." Granny O gasped. With this Justi knew she had just discovered the author, but at this moment, she found herself wishing she had not. Justi thought that Granny O had the kind of serious look that parents got when kids were in a lot of trouble.

Chapter 5

Come on everyone called Uncle Jim, it's time for the group picture. Some folks must leave soon and we need to gather for the picture while everyone is still here. It is a long-standing tradition, so everyone move along to the area right in front of the large Oak.

Before Granny O could say another word, Kate and Julie appeared to walk with her for the group picture. Granny O gave Justi a look that communicated this conversation was not over. Justi shuddered, imagining that Granny O was angry and for some odd reason, it had never occurred to Justi that was a possible reaction. In retrospect, she should have considered it the most likely reaction. She was a guest, and it turns out a nosy guest. She found a private journal and read it and exposed that fact in a tricky sort of way. *What was I thinking?* she thought to herself. It was just that the journal was so different, so unique were its contents that she wanted to know the author and talk to her. Perhaps the direct approach would have been better. Dang that hindsight!

Justi almost ran to get to the group of kids who were lining up for the picture. Jim was telling all the kids to sit down on the grass, younger ones in front and older ones in the back. He had a camera set up on a tripod a few feet back in order to get everyone in the picture. It took a while for everyone to get in place. Finally, Jim stood behind the camera and instructed some to move in, some to switch places until he could see everyone's face. He held the remote in his hand and told them he'd take several shots so to stay in place until he gave the word. Jim quickly ran and took his place in the group, then pressed the remote. Once, twice, three times. "OK, thank you everyone, we're all done!" With that word, Justi stood up and looked around for Mom and Parker. She was about to move when she felt a hand lightly touch, then squeeze her shoulder. It did not let go. She turned to face Granny O who looked at her intently and said, ""Have you been in my attic?"

"Uh, uh, yes Ma'am, I have." Justi could feel her knees shaking, but she tried not to show that she was scared. "What you found and read was written many years ago. It is private and was meant to stay that way." Justi knew she might only have one chance to get answers and it seemed she was already in trouble, so she talked as fast as she could. "I'm very, very sorry. I found it by accident. Then I read it and that was no accident, but it was so interesting, so different that curiosity got the best of me and I just couldn't wait to find and talk with the author. I assume you are she? Is it a journal or is it fiction? Are you terribly angry with me? Will you explain some of it to me? Please, please don't be mad."

Granny O sighed, "Take a breath please child, slow down! This is not the time or the place, but I do want to talk to you again. Look at me. You do not speak a word of this to anyone, understand?" Justi shook her head in agreement. And whatever you do, leave that journal in its proper place until I tell you otherwise. Granny O's words were stern and her face was serious. Justi just nodded her head. I will arrange a time to see you again. With that, Granny O turned and walked away from Justi, much faster than her 80-something legs should have allowed. Relieved to be out of trouble at least temporarily, Justi ran off to find Parker and Mom. She was now more than ready to go home.

On the ride home, Justi was mostly quiet. She couldn't stop thinking about how angry Granny O had seemed and what their next meeting might be like. Mom chattered as they drove about this relative and that and all the family news she learned. Justi couldn't help noticing that this was the most cheerful Mom had been in a long time. Perhaps Dad had been right – the change of scenery and connection to family was good for Mom.

Justi certainly had an adventure today, but it turned out to be very different than the way it had played out in her head. She had seriously miscalculated the reaction of the author. Why was Granny O so angry? Was it that Justi read her private words or was it the contents of what she'd read? Was Granny O afraid that Justi would try to do what she'd written about doing as a young girl? Or was it fiction? Really, did Granny O even remember what she'd written 60 or 70 years ago? That was a really long time to remember anything. Justi certainly had a lot of thinking to do before she saw Granny O again.

They arrived home just as the sun was starting to set. After the car was unloaded and the leftovers they'd brought with them were put away, Justi headed off to get a bath. She had a lot to think about and she wanted to get into her bed soon. She suspected she would not sleep much tonight.

Chapter 6

In the days after the family picnic, Justi stayed away from the attic. She resisted the temptation to pull the journal out and read it again. She wanted desperately to read it, this time with a different perspective. She knew the author and she wanted to write down all of her questions. However, part of her wanted to just forget the whole thing. She had broken the rules that her parents had taught her about respecting the privacy of others and she'd done it without a second thought. It had seemed to her more like an old mystery than a privacy issue. Part of her worried that Granny O would call and part of her worried that she would not call. The more time that passed, the more Justi thought Granny O was just too angry to talk to her. That made her feel both sorry and worried. She kept busy reading and playing with the neighborhood kids. She even spent some time writing in her own electronic journal, listing all of the events of the past few weeks, so she would not forget any of the details.

One afternoon Aunt Gert stopped by to visit. She told them that there was a discussion underway in the family about whether Granny O should sell this house. Bitsy thought it was just a burden to her mother, having to pay for upkeep, taxes, insurance and utilities. Granny O insisted that she just might move back there one day and that the house should remain in the family since it was a piece of history. Aunt Gert suggested that the issue might be temporarily solved if Julie and the kids decided to stay rather than return to California. Hearing this Justi was taken aback. She had enjoyed her visit, but she also looked forward to going back to school and seeing her friends. She very much wanted to go back home. She listened closely as Mom and Aunt Gert talked in the kitchen. Mom promised to email Dad to see when he thought he'd be coming home. She told Aunt Gert she appreciated the offer, but their plans had always been to return to California before Danny got back. Before leaving, Aunt Gert said that Granny O would like Justi to visit her on Friday for lunch. She should be there at 11:15

sharp. Julie's face showed that she didn't understand the invitation, but Aunt Gert said that Granny O likes to lunch with the kids one on one. It is her way of connecting with the younger generation. It is a regular event with the kids who live nearby. She will call to give Justi more information later today. Parker will have his turn unless he chooses otherwise.

On hearing this, Justi began to pace. She obviously did not get a choice in the matter. She could feel herself becoming anxious even though the lunch was two days away. She needed to think about her questions for Granny O and to really organize them she needed to look at the journal. However, Granny O was pretty clear that she should not touch the journal again. She'd just have to write her notes from memory and focus on the main themes she could remember.

After dinner on Thursday, Justi's phone dinged the sound for a new text message. She was surprised to see that she had a message from Granny O. It said:

Justi, this is Granny O. I will contact you tomorrow with instructions. You are to follow them exactly. Please confirm this message, then delete it.

Justi replied immediately with "Got it." Then she saved Granny O's phone number to her contacts and deleted the message. That night it was difficult for Justi to sleep. She kept remembering the look on Granny O's face and how dark her eyes looked. She wondered why the journal was such a secret and most of all she wondered what would happen when she was alone with Granny O and the journal.

Justi was up early the next morning. She ate breakfast, showered and dressed. She pulled her dark hair into a pony tail, then twisted it up and clipped it securely to her head. When she really needed to think, she had to have her hair out of the way. She had a feeling that she would need to think a lot today. After all these tasks were completed, the clock read eight ten. Time was certainly not flying by today. Justi hated waiting and tried to pass the time with one of her favorite video games. She had a hard time concentrating, but at least it kept her mind off the matter at hand.

At 9:00 her phone dinged and a text message popped onto the screen. It said:

Justi, get the item we discussed and place it in your pack. Do not speak to anyone about it. Bring it with you to our lunch. Be here at 11:15 am. Granny O.

Justi replied "OK" then quietly got up and got her pack from her bedroom. She took it up to the attic and sat quietly at the desk. She knew Mom was in the kitchen and she didn't want to make too much noise. Quietly, she opened the desk and found the latch that released the secret compartment. She reached in and picked up the journal. She placed it in the inside pocket of her pack so it would be safe and secure. She closed the desk, turned off the lights and went back downstairs. She kept her pack close by so she could be sure it was safe.

It seemed like two days had passed when Mom finally said it was time to go. She would drive Justi to Bitsy's house to see Granny O and drop her off. Mom chattered about how interesting Granny O was and how she just knew that Justi was going to have a great visit. She went on about how lucky Justi was to have this opportunity to spend time with Granny O and how much young people could learn from the older generation. Justi could not stop thinking that she was in trouble, this would not be fun and she was fully expecting this to be awful. She dreaded this visit, but she could not tell Mom without telling her the whole story and Granny O had been pretty clear in her instructions. Justi tried to give herself a silent pep talk. She told herself, *You can do this. Things are rarely as bad as you think. You're just a kid, what's the worst Granny O can do to you? She's had a few days to cool down. She's probably fine. She is, after all, your great-grandmother. Surely, she loves you and has gotten over being angry by now. You're a brave girl. You did not intend to offend. You are going to offer a sincere apology. That will make things OK.*

"Justi, we're here. You can get out of the car now, Mom said. I'll come to the door to find out what time to pick you up." This snapped Justi back to reality. She got out and headed up the sidewalk to Bitsy's front door. They rang the bell and Granny O showed up to answer. "Come in, Come in, she said with a smile. Julie, how about if we just call or text you a few minutes before Justi is ready. We'll have a long lunch and then a nice visit. You run along and do whatever errands you need to do. Give us plenty of time to visit." With that Julie said her good-byes and was off.

Granny O led the way down the long hallway into the kitchen. It was light and cheery with windows that looked out onto the garden. Justi could see beautiful flowers and large shade trees. There was a nice covered patio with a table and chairs. "This is a lovely house," Justi offered. Yes, it is a nice place and a nice neighborhood, but I'd still rather be in my own home. "Now, let's see about lunch. I have the table all set and ready for us to eat." So far, so good, thought Justi as she seated herself at the table across from Granny O. There was a small garden salad at each plate, a basket with warm rolls on the table and a glass of iced tea. They started to eat their salads and Granny O made small talk. Justi remembered a question and asked about the blue ceilings on porches. Granny O told her that was a special color of blue called haint blue. Haint is what some people, in this case their Pennsylvania Dutch ancestors called ghosts – haints are haunts or ghosts. Some people believed that color kept the evil spirits from entering the house. Granny O explained that she certainly didn't believe that, but for whatever reason, it is very effective at keeping the wasps and hornets from nesting on the porch. Maybe the blue makes them think they're seeing the sky. But no matter, it works. When their salads were finished, Granny O served the main course, a homemade zucchini lasagna. As they started to eat, Granny O's face became serious. She looked at Justi and said, the book you found is something I wrote many years ago, when I was probably about your age. Some of it are my memories of childhood. I was fascinated with ghosts. I wasn't scared of them, I wanted to see one. The stories cover quite a few years, and it was written by a child. It was really me recording my memories, experiences and thoughts. I never intended for anyone, especially you, to find it. It deals with a serious subject – ghosts. Not the ghosts of television and movies, but real evil.

"Could we read it together? There are some parts I didn't understand. I would like to ask questions. I'm really sorry I upset you by finding your private journal. I meant no harm. I was just so fascinated by the story that I wanted to talk with the author. I devised a plan to find try to find the author and in retrospect, I guess my plan wasn't such a good one." Granny O smiled, No, it probably wasn't. I will give you plenty of credit for creativity in your approach, though. It sure took me by surprise, but I think a more direct approach would have been easier on my old ticker. I swear child, you nearly gave me a heart attack! Let's finish our food and then perhaps I'll take a look at that old journal. My, my, I can't remember the last time I even saw it!

After lunch Justi followed Granny O outside to a set of comfortable chairs on the covered patio. Granny O explained that Bitsy was at the historical society doing her volunteer work and would not be home for several hours. Justi opened her pack, pulled out the journal and handed it to the older woman. Granny O took the book and caressed it like it was an old friend. She smiled and held it letting memories from long ago fill her mind. Slowly, she opened the book and began to read aloud.

Jan 16, 1936

Books Talk

Before I was old enough to properly express myself verbally, it occurred to me that I could think without saying anything and enjoy my own private world.

I remember sitting on my tricycle and my Mom asked what I was doing. I told her I was thinking. She told me to think on God, and I did.

I was excited about being taught to read. My parents were hopeful that I would conquer it soon, at least by my third birthday. When I couldn't pronounce a word, I would call out the letters and my Mom would respond.

What a wonderful time this was. I was discovering that there were mysteries hidden in the pages of those books. I decided to put playtime on hold. At the end of playtime what did I have? Just the end of playtime. To read and enter worlds I never knew existed I could travel and be an adventurer. Yes! And still be home in time for dinner and wonder some more.

At dinner my Dad mentioned that a blizzard may be headed our way, but they hoped it would by-pass us. He was concerned because we were due to go out of state in the morning, and the trip could not be postponed. A phone call later led me to believe it was to attend a funeral.

In the morning the snow flurries were enough to delight any child; and leaving when it was still dark outside was even better. As daylight approached, the winds increased by no blizzard appeared. It was a long journey. As we were entering the city I could see the church. It looked like a picture with the snow falling softly.

Once inside I was told to sit still in my seat and not to turn around. I promptly did as I was told.

When the service was over, the Priest came over to talk to Dad and his brothers. Then suddenly the Priest asked if he could help me. I was so surprised I frowned, not fully understanding, I said yes and that I wanted to see the Holy Ghost!

He made it perfectly clear that it was not possible, so I asked to see the Holy Ghost's mother and on being told that wouldn't be arranged either, I simply wanted to know if the Holy Ghost had been naughty and if that was why I couldn't see him.

The Priest turned to my Dad and said that I should be in school. In my defense, my Dad said that I was only three. The Priest remarked, "yes, three and full of questions. " My Dad thanked him, but I didn't understand why because he didn't help. I didn't get to see the Holy Ghost.

That evening after dinner and talk about the deceased was over, the conversation was about ghosts. Many took turns reliving their experiences and claiming this very house was haunted. Family members asked my Dad why I wasn't afraid of ghosts. Dad said I just wasn't and perhaps it was because I hadn't seen one. I looked forward to the deceased's return any minute. The evening ended and no ghost arrived.

Justi interrupted, "Granny O, you really wanted to see a ghost? You weren't afraid of them?" No, I guess I was a little like you, Justi, just naturally curious. "You weren't three when you wrote this?" No, of course not, I was writing about something that happened when I was three, I was probably ten or twelve at the time I wrote this. Ok, please go on, Justi urged.

Jan 22, 1936

Learning

It was good to be home again. Perhaps hidden somewhere in the books I'd find a formula on how to make a ghost appear. As time goes by I will keep on searching for the answers, never dismissing them from my mind.

Maybe the question I have been asking is wrong, and that's why the answer is wrong. Hearing about ghosts is not the answer. I need to see one for myself.

If it's true that people die and return after death, why don't they talk? They used to talk. The pieces of the puzzle just don't fit.

I have to get back to my reading. There was this man, Socrates, and he fascinates me. He believed in reasoning and discussion of a subject and arriving at a logical answer. I tried this on my Mom, but she reasoned right back with me that flashlights were for searching for lost items, emergencies or power failure. They were not for reading under the covers. I agreed. After all, she was declaring exactly what I had come to believe in. I had to put Socrates, one of the great minds of the Western world, on hold until tomorrow. This proved to be most painful because I remembered that Malachi, the last prophet of the Old Testament had been called the Socrates of the prophets because he used that style that specialists in rhetoric call dialectic or simply the questions and answer system to help him rule the people.

Although I am thankful for our small home library, to me it seems overflowing and tantalizing and super great in quality. No words appear to be wasted. The time I spend reading reveals to me the continuity of the knowledge I never knew existed – and how one bit of information leads to more and my cup is bubbling over.

I began to notice how worn the cover on the dictionary is. Now I've come to the conclusion that it was in great demand by the entire family.

Little did I know how great a "tool of the trade" it actually was. So far, the dictionary is the only tool I have at my disposal. To find out that Noah Webster spent 27 years of his life to compile his version was amazing to me. That was back in 1806. The dictionary by Robert Cawdrey written in 1604, only copy known to exist is at the Bodleian Library in Oxford, England. That is what I call preservation. Maybe all dictionaries weren't so reliable but in 1775 Samuel Johnson's, A *Dictionary of the English Language* was known to be just that. All the dates are amazing to have happened so long ago and yet these men had such an inner drive and so unselfishly brought about definitions that they just couldn't see lost in the passing of time, and I praise them for that.

To top it all off, I found out that an archeologist from the University of Chicago, founded the Chicago Oriental Institute and was responsible for unearthing the oldest dictionary ever discovered. In 1921, in Ebla, today known as Syria, from the Akkadian Empire, cuneiform clay tablets, James Henry Breasted found these to be dated about 2300 BCE. These were so well preserved they could be deciphered. I marvel at the fact that skilled workers had such excellent craftsmanship centuries ago.

I would also like to know how they defined "ghost." Most dictionaries that I have knowledge of list it as a spirit or a human who died and reappeared as a ghost, Ghost, I believe we just might have a rendezvous. Also, let it be known that if you believe the struggle availeth not may I inform you that you don't know me! I was not born to patience but I possess something better. It has a name. Its name is endurance!

February 5, 1936

An Experience

Can't waste any more time. Just have to call a meeting of self. Oh these ghosts! How did they get so organized? Who taught them? Where did they learn so much? Did they go to school after they died? I know this much: I've heard family members and friends say the ones who passed on didn't make good grades in school. The talk at funerals and family gatherings tells me that many were not organized. One thing I recall loud and clear – they could talk. Better still you could understand them. When described by family members, the difference of when they were with us is not the same as now. When family approach them, they back off like crawdads. The children they loved don't smile, but run away. No resemblance of their former self.

The strangest thing of all is the reaction of pets. They back off and their hair stands up and barking and meowing, they dance sideways. I want to know why. I just heard the sound that signifies dinner is ready. As I came past the door, the neighborhood children were announcing their plans to go to the movies to see a cowboy picture. They were reminding me that I said I liked Westerns. It was funny because I seem to be attracted to Westerns- past and present.

At dinner, again the talk was about a short journey tomorrow afternoon and home by evening. Dad inquired about my studies and was I thinking about being an archeologist. I told him I thought perhaps I'd do my digging in the books and that would keep me busy long enough; that is until I found that idea or better still that hidden formula for locating a ghost. The answer just had to be in there somewhere. Before I was here wasn't there someone else on earth who wondered about ghosts and asked the same questions I'm asking now? Of course, there had to be. I am not the "Lone Ranger" or am I? Again, here goes the question and answer game again. Couldn't I have chosen a different subject to be interested in? How is it that I think as I do? Maybe it all adds up to the fact that I am alone and no one is in this library studying but me. I am the only one in this class. I'm in this class by myself and the only one to reason with and discuss things with is me. On the other hand, if someone in the past had found the answer where oh where could the little answer be? The question was little when I first wanted an answer. Now it is so big. Where is the big book that has it recorded? There are no big books in here. Could it be true that big things have been known to come in little packages!

As dinner was almost over, my mom suggested that I give the books a rest. I said I'd think it over. Our dinner guest, a friend and neighbor was silent all through dinner, until now. She asked what grade I was in. I told her I was busy at the "dig" in our library. As I asked to be excused, she said she hoped I found something. Maybe I just did! Remembering she had asked about a grade, sure, for ghosts in their new existence maybe they are in different grades. As I left the dining room I heard someone asking my mom about the correct temperature to bake bread. Mom's reply was the degree was very important

If the degree was so important for bread it could be the same for ghosts, maybe considering how they performed. A number one, two or three. Better still first, second and third degree, that sounds more ghostly. Yes!

By the next afternoon the weather was warmer and our trip was short and pleasant. All I could think about was a ghost with a degree. A third degree ghost probably had been around longer and had more power.

"Granny O, Justi exclaimed, you were a girl detective too!" Well, yes, I suppose I was. Granny O returned her attention to the journal and read:

Our trip was almost over and we stopped at the town square that Dad said was so special. I didn't see anything special about it. There was a grocery store and out in front some tree stumps and chairs and men sitting and leaning back on their chairs and some were sleeping. Dad had a delivery to make and we waited for him. When he came back he was carrying the local newspaper and asked if we'd like to look around and get something to drink. My mom went in the store but I stayed outside. I wanted to know what was so special about this place. When I asked Dad he said you could learn a lot here and that it was interesting. I told him Mom would make these men sit up straight and get busy. They were idle. The only thing anyone was doing was the man carving on a cane. Whoa! Dad picked me up and stood me on a tree stump and told me in no uncertain terms that these men weren't idle. The men I thought were sleeping, were praying and Dad said that is what was holding this old world together.

About that time, the man carving gave me a whistle. Just made out of a plain old piece of wood and he left that little loose piece in the middle so it would sound. I thanked him for the treasure. I learned things weren't always as they appeared. I was sorry I misjudged.

All the way home I held that whistle remembering it had come from a place that was so special. Most of all I was thankful for the prayers that were holding our world together. Just Imagine how powerful prayers are!

March 5, 1936

Neutral

In my pursuit of ghosts, am I to believe that through the centuries a correct description of ghosts would be humans who had lived and died and came back to receive the reward of becoming eligible for "ghost-hood?" Then and only then could they obtain an Evilution License to haunt!

Granny O, interrupted Justi, "I've never heard of Evilution before. What is it?" It is a term I made up to describe the evil that happens when ghosts are eligible for ghost-hood, which something else I made up. It seemed to me back then, and I guess it is true today that ghosts were evil spirits, so I named their becoming a ghost Evilution. That is clever said Justi. I like the term. I'm sorry for interrupting, please continue. Granny O nodded and began to read again.

And haunt and haunt, and for what purpose? To become more and more miserable than they were before death? Which way is it? Causing agony and sorrow. Where is their rest and longed for peace of mind? Just can't have it both ways. I thought they were supposed to wait until Judgment Day. Don't they ever complain? They appear to be on a journey to nowhere. Whatever we might think of them, they are here. It is as if they are saying, now you see me, now you don't. We are independent but we'll freely tell you this – *we feel. No explanation necessary* – so you prove it – what you think we're not. However silent, this comes across perfectly. You know when you wanted an answer from your Mom and Dad and they didn't even look at you. Ok, you got it. Obviously, you should have known better than to have asked. Their silent message was – no explanation necessary.

When I realize I have been challenged, I know the time has come to take inventory. Check all my tools to see what I need. Am I sure I am ready? Well, first, all I have is a hungry mind and my books.

It has never occurred to me that I couldn't find the answer I so desperately seek if I just don't give up. In the past, I thought perhaps I should let it go. But, not now. A challenge is a demand for an explanation, according to my tool as it speaks out, even though silently, it speaks. What a tool of the trade this dictionary is!

Let it be known, loud and clear, I have no intention of folding my tent and silently stealing away. At one time, I ran from play into the house and my Mom asked why I left playing kick the can in the alley when I still had play time left. I told her they were fighting and I didn't want to take sides. She told me that no daughter of hers would ever be classed as neutral. Even though I said I might be beaten up and I didn't know what they were fighting about. She told me to go and choose a side and I did and I got beaten up because I had never fought before.

When I came back in the door she just looked at me and smiled. I knew then I could never sit on top of the fence. No neutrality for me.

Even though I had learned the hard way, in the future I would choose a side.

Listening and obeying was so much a part of my life a few bumps and bruises were kind of like badges. I wore them proudly!

Back now to the inventory which seems lacking Perhaps, very lacking but not when you put some force behind it and push. Now considering the fact that I have been challenged and having arrived at logic I can forget the bumps and bruises. The results when proven right, just might have a tendency to be overwhelming.

Remember I am not one to sit on top of the fence. I am taking my stand. Since I have been informed that this is a true declaration of war, I am declaring right back.

I will answer the ghosts officially. As Rene Descartes has stated, "I think, therefore I am." I am ready and I am explaining that I understand the challenge. This is the "war of words." No matter how I managed to get here, maybe through desperation, frustration or imagination or all three, I am here. Even though I am self-appointed, I have arrived.

Being challenged I didn't know not to answer. I never questioned it then and I'm not questioning it now.

It is obvious that having ventured out on uncharted water, the little child in me is speaking out, while searching through the fog of time. Rest assured I go not blindly. As I wonder, I will talk to "self" and rely on the question and answer system for the logic. Here goes, "self"

"Hello"

If you are awake I can talk to you. If you are asleep, I might awaken you. If you are dead, being the optimist that I am, I could possibly revive you. If you are complacent, then it could prove to be far more difficult. That would require renewal!

Once the inner self has been awakened, oh! There lies the mystery and I might add within reach. The long awaited looms more clearly now. Let the revelation begin.

March 15, 1936

Supervision

It was obvious, especially to my parents, that even at such an early age, I needed privacy. With visitors coming in and out they invariably sought me out, so for the rest of the day, I avoided the library. To visitors I was a curiosity. To my parents I was an ordinary child who was content to spend time reading for herself.

Stringing beans was one thing I did very well. Hearing them snap as I broke them meant I was making progress. There was a bushel to take care of and it made me feel needed. No complaints from this helper. My Mom said she didn't want to make too great a demand on me, so she planned breaks. We didn't stop working, just changed to another task and emptied waste baskets, checked the mail at the front porch mailbox, folded towels, put a napkin at each place for dinner and helped choose flowers from the garden to brighten the buffet.

It is strange how words spoken cling to your mind and you hear them later on running around in your head. I never realized until now that there are different ways you can make demands. You can demand silently, quietly or forcefully. I'll reserve my silent ones for me! Quiet ones for those around me and forceful ones for the appointment I expect to happen. I am now creating my formula to present to ghost. It consists of what I like and I am expressing myself out loud. I have knowledge of the fact that ghosts are not capable of reading your mind. That is unless you let them. I have no intention of doing that, because what I'd say would no longer be a surprise to them. I will keep repeating what I like. I do not want there to be any doubt about the fact that I like Monks and monasteries. Monks are to be admired. They pray, work and earn money with the sale of articles they produce. They do not waste time and they are devout in their worship of Almighty God. They do not have to explain why they have chosen their profession. Their behavior speaks for itself. I will continue to pray for them. As days speed into months, I will make it known out loud that any extra money I get I will donate it joyfully to the monks. After all, their prayers are holding this old world together.

Tomorrow, I am in hopes that I can read and search some more. I intend to stay focused. I like to dream of success and to wonder how it will feel to accomplish a mission. I know there is a chance of success and a chance of the alternative. I do not entertain those negative thoughts. I seek to uncover the truth. I feel it is under a cloud of mistaken identity.

Let it be known that my theory is not based on chance but solely on logic. Yes, I have designed this formula using my mind, Bible, dictionary and other books in my small library. The comfort of family who grant me space with supervision and have complete respect for what I do, knowing I need time to wonder and dream. Time to express my thoughts in private. I am surrounded with the best in literature and the freedom to concentrate and arrive at my own conclusions. This is a healthy atmosphere.

I dare say that I have a valid reason for this experiment, previously untried. There is no record so far as anyone attempting this. You may think it too simple to bring results. I look at it in a different way. The far-fetched complicated ways have never brought out what I believe is hidden.

We must take into consideration my not being "an individual of letters." I can advance at the only pace I know, one step at a time. Monks with all due respect, please keep praying!

March 18, 1936

Hideaway

As dawn was breaking I was awakened by a noise overhead. As I hurried out of bed, Mom called me to come to the attic. What a mess! She was rearranging things so I could have my books up there to give me some privacy. The end part of the attic would be perfect because I could adjust the sliding window for fresh air.

The slate blackboard, desk and chair would be helpful. During the early evening the gooseneck lamp would brighten any corner. I couldn't bring all the books up, just the ones I use the most. My bible, a small dictionary, the set of *Great Minds of the Western World,* Shakespeare, poetry and world history would do for now. Once they were arranged and the floor cleaned, I put down the throw rugs including the sheep skin, a favorite of mine. What a welcome change this will be, privacy beyond compare. A secret hideaway with my own key. Now I can lock the door from the inside and only Mom has a matching key. What a morning this has been.

"Privacy interjected Justi, is why I went to your attic in the first place, Granny O. I needed a quiet place, away from Parker and Mom to do my thinking. I didn't know that same attic was your private place, too!" Granny O replied, "Yes, having a quiet place with privacy can help the thought process immensely I spent a lot of time in that attic all by myself, thinking, reading and writing. " And trying to make a ghost appear? asked Justi. Granny O nodded silently and continued.

All the family will be in at noon. Lunch time is always exciting. News from school and work is never dull. Mom and I had to hurry to set the table. Timing is everything. When all were seated and grace was said, Dad turned to me and asked where his instruction booklet was - the one on fishing lures. I told him I had it and I'd return it to his nightstand. I liked helping with the assembly parts of lures and I changed and rearranged the process. Sure was better when my idea caused the fish to rush to it. Dad was kind to let me figure it my way. I hadn't progressed enough to paint them yet. I was told that would come later, so would my learning to cast. Dad just said weather permitting, we might go camping tomorrow. He had a co-worker ready to fill in and be on call for Saturday and Sunday.

When lunch was over, Mom handed me the basket with supplies to take to the attic. It contained my flashlight with extra batteries, paper, pencils, chalk, a new eraser for the blackboard, a small waste basket and a box of tissues. She also reminded me that I was to return the booklet on lures. She offered an explanation for having removed the sign my brother had on the attic door when he was assembling his model airplane. Her opinion was that signs are known to attract attention and create curiosity. I valued her opinion. It showed wisdom so, explanation accepted.

At dinner Dad gave instructions to my brothers about what gear to pack. My sisters were in charge of assisting Mom with the preparation of our food supplies. My duty was to be sure all the flashlights had the right size batteries and extra wicks for the lanterns. I was also in charge of the empty kerosene cans by placing them in the crates. The matches had cans to keep them dry. First aid supplies needed to be organized. I was a jumper, you know, always ready to fetch and carry whatever I was called on to do. My brothers said they had gotten me the canteen but had forgotten the collar, guessed that was the reason I never wore it – precisely!

I reminded Dad to pick up extra batteries for his radio. Now, if only the weather would cooperate. The camp site had originally been Dad's friend's private cabin where he entertained his buddies. When he was no longer a bachelor, he maintained it in good order and let his buddies take turns camping there.

It was late when Dad came home. My brothers were at camp running the lines so we would have fresh fish tomorrow. I looked up at Dad and remarked that the sky was red tonight, sailor's delight. Tomorrow should be just fine.

March 19, 1936

Camping

Arriving at the camp site at noon, after unloading, it seemed as if nothing had been forgotten. All appears peaceful. I was not prepared for what happened next.

A young man ran toward us panting and trying to talk at the same time and yelling that he was not going back. My brothers told him to calm down and sit down and rest and we weren't going to make him do anything. A little later he was offered a drink.

The camp fire was in the center so all of us could gather around. The coffee was perking, the frying pan was over the fire and the corn in the husk was on the wood coals. The filets of fish were on ice. Wood smoke and the aroma of coffee filled the air. Our family was gathering in close with everyone helping. Still, a feeling of tension was in the air. With the fish ready and all the side dishes set out, the invitation to eat all you can was extended and left-overs would not be tolerated.

Even if the weather changed, we were prepared. We could spend the night in the cabin already reserved for us, and we could breakfast inside just fine. The men went to check the fishing lines and the girls were cleaning up along with burning the paper products. Things seemed to be in order with the exception of our visitor.

It was after nine and Dad came running to tell us that the radio announcer had sent out a warning that an electrical storm with high winds was 30 minutes to an hour away. The car headlights would give us enough light to get from the campfire to the cabin. We could be indoors safe with time to spare.

The move was fast. We turned the lantern on just in case the power went off. We were all in except the men and our visitor. As soon as the men returned they went right back out the door to look for him. They found him by the remains of the campfire. All were indoors now. Suddenly, the power went off. The lanterns were turned up while everyone was getting seated.

Our visitor apologized for acting the way he did, but said if we had seen the "ghost" he saw we would have run too. He claimed he had never seen one before and he jumped around trying to avoid it, then it pushed him. He said when he was swinging at it his fist went right through its chest and the ghost vanished.

By now the fireplace was ready to light the wood and the wood cook stove was heating up. Time was right for coffee and hot chocolate. The girls were busy filling cups, placing them on the big picnic table in the center of the room. Everyone could help themselves. To our visitor, Dad said, "it's time we know who you are," then paused, waiting on his response. Our visitor had the look of a frightened child. He kept looking around and behind him. We all heard the latch on the front door click as it was lifted, but no one came in. Dad motioned for silence and it was as if time stood still. Then a thud and the door opened back with a bang. A voice called out that they tried to get our attention. Thought they had better pull out our fishing lines in order to save them. Informed us that they last time the creek flooded it took everything in its path. Told us we had better move our cars. Offered to sound their siren and ring the big bell if the cabin was in danger. With the door left standing open they were gone out of sight. Dad called out a thank you, but no reply.

With the fish in buckets and the fishing gear pulled out of the way, Dad closed the door. By now the wind was howling and the fog and rain were running a race. It was doubtful that even a ghost would enter our domain. Dad turned up the radio. It was safe to say that the storm would last through the night.

It was past midnight now. The bunks were built up against the wall, upper and lower. Paired in fours. Sixteen in all. One bed with no bunk was by the front wall by the door. Guess dad was due to nap there. Our visitor spoke out and said his name was anything we chose it to be. Claimed he was an orphan and never knew his name. He said at first he thought the people across the hill were playing a joke on him, but when the ghost had no body to hit and vanished he knew then it wasn't a joke. But he couldn't understand why it pushed him. There were no murmurs to be heard. Only sounds were the thunder and rain beating down on the tin roof and the fireplace making little popping sounds. What was to become of our visitor? He deserved a name. A proper name. I was sad for him. I wanted to see a ghost and he feared one would see him. I know more now than I did – about ghosts that is!

March 25, 1936

Gone Fishin'

I love fishing and everything that goes with it. Digging worms, seining minnows, helping make bait. Every time I hear talk about a new bait recipe I make a copy and put it in my file box. It is true, my box only contains fish bait recipes. I don't know what else a file box is supposed to be used for. Of all the recipes I have, I like preparing this one best of all. I wouldn't mind sharing it, but no one in my age group is interested in fishing. They offer to go fishing with us if I'll bait the hook and take the fish off. That's watching. Fishing isn't for everyone.

Sometimes when I'm out on the back patio assembling the fish bait ingredients the neighborhood children are observing from a distance. They complain the mixture smells bad. It's only absorbent cotton mixed with limburger cheese. The cheese has to be room temperature or it won't mix. Just make little balls about the size of a marble and put them in a metal can with a tight fitting lid. Then comes the good part. You have to dig a hole and bury the can. It is best if left two or more weeks. When you dig it up, you don't open it until you're out fishing. Then it smells really bad. The fish love it. Not only do bottom feeders go for it, but quite a variety of others.

Due to the fact that I have taken a stand in search of the truth, I pretend I am casting in hopes that I've chosen the right lure so I'll reel in the key. That key will give me more courage to venture forth in full pursuit of the lock and the container that is withholding those valuables. I wonder how long they have been locked away. Could it be they are not disguised at all? Could it be by word of mouth the truth has been lost in repetition? You know a story passed from person to person and at the end it is not the same story at all! The story from ancient times is the same as now. A person who has lived and died and then returned as a ghost! Or it could be a spirit. First, I'll have to expect the one that used to be human. It certainly seems to be more popular. I keep repeating that

I like monks and monasteries and when I come into money, inherited or otherwise, I'll contribute just like I promised.

I have more time now that I have the hideaway. I can leave and come back and find things just as I left them. Pick up right where I left off. Something seems different. I left my jacket hanging on the back of my chair and it's hanging on the hook on the back of the door. I'll put it back on the chair and be more careful next time. I am a creature of habit. Shoes by the door, taken off as soon as I lock the door from the inside. The rugs stay clean longer and they feel so good to walk on. Dinner will be a little late tonight. I will have the extra time to check the downstairs library for the *Time and Space Books.*

Dad is teaching me about the stars, galaxies and the sun and the moon. The pictures in the books match the ones in the heavens. I find it hard to believe, just like the church did in 1633, that the earth moves around the sun. Galileo believed it and was denounced to the Inquisition, imprisoned and forced to recant. Legend has it that even as he publicly denied that the earth moved, he muttered to himself, "and yet it moves!" The church later publicly announced that they had made a mistake. In setting the record straight I discovered that Galileo's family moved to Florence, Italy in the 1570's and he began his formal education at a school in a nearby monastery. Appears he was taught very well. I'll continue to need more help studying the heavens. I could spend the night in the hammock just looking up at the heavens.

Dad is working on our new telescope, and I am excited because it's going to be far more powerful that the one we have now. The lenses are expensive but hopefully we'll sell enough lures to cover part of the cost. Dad is also building a bigger tripod that rotates, so we'll be ready to mount the new telescope in time to see the northern lights from our own back yard.

Just heard the sound that dinner is ready. It's going to be different tonight. Everything is home made. Barbeque, buns and root beer. We made the root beer months ago and I learned to use the bottle capper. When this batch is gone, we'll make another one. This is what I call a party!

When dinner was over we sat on the lawn to study the heavens. It was getting cooler so I hurried to the attic to get my jacket. I just couldn't find it. I know I put it on the back of my chair. It wasn't on the hook on the door either. Then I saw it hanging on the window latch. At least I found it. I must have put it there by accident as I was closing the window.

April 10, 1937

Rendezvous

I find it interesting that a man who lived in the 400s BC is credited with writing these words that are inscribed on the Central Post Office building in New York City:

"Neither snow nor rain nor heat nor gloom of night stays these couriers from the swift completion of their appointed rounds."

Herodotus, a Greek historian described the postal messengers of the Persian empire based in what is now Iran for their swiftness regardless of the weather to deliver the messages and packages by runner or couriers on horseback, travelling swiftly, sometimes more than one hundred miles a day using relay stations.

After learning this I am more determined that my goal cannot be forgotten.

I like monks and I like monasteries. I will give sleep a vacation. I have a rendezvous to keep. I feel that I have made progress and that I am on the threshold of a discovery, delayed though it has been.

When I read of people from the past and what they have endured to accomplish near impossible tasks, I marvel at their determination. There seemed to be no limit as to what they were expected to do. It more or less left the door wide open for success, and succeed they did.

My thoughts keep spinning around and constantly reminding me that I can reach my goal if I just don't give up; No matter how many times I get side tracked or others try to influence me to change my cause of action, I rebel and I seclude myself and proceed full speed ahead. I know when the forces are drawing me and opening my mind to pursue new avenues, there is no turning back.

I am aware that I am growing up and new demands are being made on my time. One thing I know I can depend on is change. Change is good. Regardless of how things change, I will cling to the basics and keep things simple.

Simplicity proves to be most helpful when you are creating a formula or unraveling one.

I do spend a lot of time alone, to fathom and come to an understanding of the true identity of what a ghost actually is. To others this may not seem to be an important issue, but to me it is.

As I sit here in the living room alone in the lounge chair, calmly saying in just a whisper, "I like monks and I like monasteries," I picture in my mind's eye of strolling down a corridor in a monastery and of the peace and serenity found there.

I am writing about what a ghost is and is not.

Suddenly I am poked two times in my right shoulder. As I looked up there was a huge monk – very large hands and very large solid white finger nails, no moons. He is dressed in a gown and robe off white in color. His arms and hands out stretched. In his hands he is clutching vials. His hair is long and thin. I am aware someone, not as tall, is behind him. I just got a glimpse of his off-white robe.

They spoke not a word. The way the huge monk was holding out the vials, I thought he wanted me to reach for them. As I reached, my hands and arms went through his hands and arms as I was ready to pull back with the vials, both disappeared.

I was surprised, but not afraid. Instantly I looked straight ahead and I saw three more monks. They were smaller and the tallest was in the rear and he had on a tan robe with the hood up. The middle one had on an off-white robe, no hood. The one in the front was shorter and his robe was off-white. As he stepped forward he nodded and held out a large dusty green paper. It was written in bronze colored ink. It had a bronze border all around. My name was on it and I knew it was a check with many, many numbers.

As I leaned forward to get a better look, it vanished and so did they.

I was remembering the monk with the tan hooded robe because he smiled at me. The large monk walked with a distinctive lunge to the left and right. Not a sound, only complete silence. Just exactly what did I see? I need some time to evaluate this. I anticipated their arrival. Because there were five instead of one was not confusing. It was the appearance of the ghosts themselves!

I did not see a loved one or a friend. There was nothing personal about their visit. They did not make a sign, write a note or inquire about anyone. A human who returned would attempt some kind of gesture in search of someone they had known.

They were not monks. They were dressed to appear like monks, but they were mimics. They were impostors. They carried vials to let me know they were capable of sending out fragrances or aromas. Offering a check when I am aware that monks are not in the business of handing out checks.

The one in the hooded robe, smiling to get my attention to let me know he had on the robe associated with monks because I said I liked monks, they appeared as "ghosts by design." It might seem like a case of mistaken identity but it was definitely not. There were no ex-humans involved here.

Justi looked a little scared, but remained silent. She would hold her questions for later. Granny O continued.

April 12, 1937

Revelation

A ghost, is a ghost, is a ghost! When is a ghost not a ghost? There is never a time that a ghost is not a ghost!

I followed my formula step by step and it happened-ghosts appeared. Not that my approach was noteworthy, nor did I present a master plan. Just a simple formula.

Now concerning ghosts-what they think is their island is not their island at all. It is their prison. Being spirit imprisoned – only spirits can free them, but that is not possible. Spirits are too weak. Even though spirits can convince, deceive and mimic, cause heat and cold to be felt, aromas and fragrances to fill the air, touch and move objects and be mobile, shockingly enough, spirits are very lacking.

The ghosts everyone seems to be so familiar with, are evil spirits. They are not an apparition. That is not their title. They are not a disembodied entity.

How did I arrive at this decision? To be disembodied you had to have had a body. They never did. The ghosts that appeared to me were not the soul or spirit of a human who had lived and died and returned to earth.

As familiar as I was with the Holy Scriptures, I had to wonder was there something I had missed because of all the talk about ghosts and their many followers. Humans who passed on and returned, would not have followers. It did seem right for evil spirits, so I am happy to reveal that the living need not be concerned over their loved ones or friends who have passed on. It just so happens when you leave this earth your spirit goes back to the God who gave it and is in another dimension and your spirit does not return to earth. There is no record of anyone in the past who has ever returned as a ghost, no one in the present day and no one is being expected to be in the future. It is written. The Holy Scriptures do not lie.

From time immemorial, rushing through the centuries, many humans who have haunted businesses have felt fortunate to state that their property has been termed "haunted," having paranormal activity." They have been delighted to hang out their sign. To be validated makes it legitimate, so to speak. After all, "ghosts mean money!"

Now they can join the caravan of their fellow colleagues operating the same business in which they are so devotedly engaged.

Let it be known they still have their ghosts. They are evil spirits pretending to be ex-humans. They have proved to be excellent at haunting. Fooled multitudes so far.

Those in business can secretly or openly express their opinion if they hold the belief that ghosts are deceased humans, or they can rest assured that ghosts are the evil ones, not disembodied entities.

Finally, as I experienced it, your home, businesses or establishments are truly haunted, no bones about it! As we all know, "flesh and bones" do not a ghost make.

Sign (Imagined Only)

Come one! Come all!

We entertain angels!

Yes, they're fallen- but look where they've been

"Right from heaven itself"

You just might see them floating around

Switching on lights- moving objects

They're here- plenty of them

Fragrant breezes – "hear footsteps?"

Establishment Answers

Did I hear you say evil spirits?

You can hear all kinds of things!

1. They do no harm
2. Sure don't take up space
3. Come on, see for yourself
4. We're envied because of much activity here
5. We have proof
6. Guess that makes us professionals now
7. Only ghosts and only ours
8. Spend the night-room service available & more
9. Open on weekends
10. Lunch on premises
11. Tours available
12. Guides on hand
13. We've been rated
14. Paranormal activity here
15. Memorabilia
16. Parties – we reserve
17. Large Parties – book ahead
18. Satisfaction guaranteed
19. We guarantee friendly ghosts
20. Cameras welcome
21. Our ghosts have names
22. Sit on their own tombstones – sometimes
23. In dress of "time they lived"
24. Soldiers in uniform
25. Ghost photos available
26. We have spirits and loved ones
27. All ghosts welcome
28. Sea Captains cruise in

Establishment Comments

Yes, they are evil, at least some are, but no one is perfect.

Think about it, we've all made mistakes~

If they were perfect some wouldn't be here, now would they?

"Let's Party"

"For future reference"

"So, let me get this straight, said Justi. There are ghosts, they are real, but they are not what we think of as ghosts, someone who died that has come back to haunt. They are some kind of evil spirits. This is what you termed as Evilution earlier?" Yes, that is correct answered Granny O. Even today, people still believe ghosts are what Hollywood tells us, but that is not true. Ghosts are evil spirits who were never human. Justi felt a cold shiver go done her spine. This was just as scary as she remembered. Justi took a deep breath. Please continue she said.

April 15, 1937

Fakes

In the process of unravelling my formula, I fear not to relate my findings. In the past, the writers of the dictionaries picked up on what the ancients feared. Fear kept alive the legend of the ghosts. A legend is a popular unverified story handed down from earlier times. The ancients, assuming ghosts were the dead returned, and with the evil spirits mimicking the deceased, actually increased fears all the more. Even now, I choose to investigate the definition of the dead returned as ghosts because they were more popular.

After encountering ghosts who dressed "by design," proved to me to be beyond a doubt "fakes." It left only one alternative, "a spirit and a thought to be ex-human ghost" were one and the same. There were not two choices. Realizing now the simplicity of it all, the ancients, in their fear saying they had seen something pass by that was shaped like a person, the evil spirits were quick to reappear and let the ancients assume they had guessed correctly.

I only did the talking hoping to attract them. It worked to my advantage, not the ghosts'.

First, my jacket was moved around a lot. During the early afternoon, not at dark, they appeared. Not as friend or relative, but exactly as the ones I spoke of, monks.

I know now how well they can hear and I do wonder, do they always mimic what they hear spoken? About that I do not know, except it worked that way for me.

I didn't give up and I have been rewarded. I sought the truth for me and I am willing to share! As I was travelling through my books, I was comforted to find it written that "truth alone triumphs." What an inscription, what a motto for a nation- India, Thank You!

It actually comes down to this. It is a battle of good versus evil. There is a devil and he rules the world. I never knew until now how evil spirits entered humans physically and mentally causing them to become greedy and destructive.

The ghosts have exposed one way. If you invite ghosts in or find them in your home and voice no objection to them because they do you no harm, don't take up space, you are catering to them. In so doing, you are leaving the door wide open for them to control you! Regardless of this you will still wonder why they don't talk. I've given that a lot of thought. Why should they? They don't have to. Remember, they are in control.

They haven't talked since who knows when and not so they can be understood. Why should they "rock the boat "now?

They appear to be flaunting their independence. Ghosts, the ones I saw didn't deliver. It is for sure they did appear!

Their actions spoke so loudly, had they spoken, I wouldn't have heard a word they said! They insulted my intelligence by offering me a check and definitely underestimated me in general. The child in me seeks out little details and things that don't fit. The monk's attire, the smile and having more than one monk appear. There shouldn't have been any monks at all if they were who they were pretending to be. I was not shocked. I was too busy observing. Idle they were. Had they been busy doing their duty, only one would have appeared and not in monk attire! They were idle impostors.

Granny O paused and looked up from the journal to reassure Justi. "Rest assured we have power over them, dear. We can demand them to leave and they will go. Even in the past and up until now we have neglected exercising this power.

With no need to fear we can demonstrate our power of control over them. When they rebelled in heaven and chose Satan as their master, their spirits being cast away, they lost the privilege of the ability to materialize and dematerialize their body, and to think they had a résumé to be envied. Fellowship in heaven with the Highest. What an education, what an experience and what an existence!

It was not ambition that drove them to sin, it was greed and envy. Now they have been known to bring down kingdoms. The perils they are responsible for are legion! I am not the one to take this title from them. They have earned it! So much for their destruction. I'll just leave them to heaven!"

I guess that makes me feel a little better said Justi. Please keep reading.

April 26, 1937

Reality – Relief

All is not lost! I may not be the one, such as Paul Revere, who made the midnight ride to sound the alarm of approaching enemies, and I was not there when the shot fired was heard 'round the world, but I am here now and so are the enemies!

I do not take lightly being spied on day and night by evil spirits. These are not "peeping toms," they dwell within our homes. I do not intend to look the other way. This is not the "Emperor's Empire" where "fear" reigns supreme. There is a battle going on here and I highly resent my privacy being invaded!

Being surrounded by untold numbers of evil spirits means hauntings will be increasing. It is a sure sign that it is a ghost's way of letting us know they want us "out!" They have this desire to replace us! Why? They can't control us! That in itself is good news! I won't settle for good news when great can be had!

Columbus discovered the new world in a simple undecked boat.

Napoleon conquered Europe by resorting to a temporary encampment and fell back on courage, boldness and bravery all from within himself.

When I started my journey, it never occurred to me that <u>my mind, voice and determination</u> might not be sufficient!

Odd isn't it - that help would arrive in such a strange manner? It didn't come in a big way, but it did come and aroused a longing in me to seek the truth and even provided the strength to endure. Help from within, a truly mysterious visitor, and a welcome one!

I wonder, why did it take so long to learn that ghosts are evil spirits? Now that it's known, will it be ignored? The Emperor had his reason concerning the evil pretend weavers. He feared being classed as stupid. Today, it's still "fear." There are some living who fear that the ghosts will leave. These evil ones have no intention of doing that. They will be more popular than ever.

Remember, "Ghost means money!"

Of the modern ghost stories, Joseph Sheridan Le Fanu, Irish author wrote his first ghost story in 1838 and ghost talk is still going on today. The golden age of ghost stories was in the 1800s in England.

Justi thought about this and said, "Not much has changed since you wrote this, has it? Television, movies, books and a whole lot of conversations are over-flowing with the ghosts' popularity. People still don't understand what you learned as a girl about ghosts, do they?" That is a good observation, Justi.

They are the same ghosts as before. The message that I am conveying is simple. Looking deeper into this and beyond the places where paranormal activity is happening, be it private residences or a business would lead you to believe that being left with only one definition of ghost "ghost= evil spirit" would be a disappointment to the living who have suffered the loss of loves ones and friends. Not so! Label it "relief." It appears to be a blessing that has been disguised too long. Not anymore.

Evil spirits though they be, are still haunting. People who have liked having them around might not be aware of the full meaning and advantages that are occurring here.

Just what does it mean having ghosts around? It is nothing new. We need to approach it in a different manner. They have been here for centuries. Long before we arrived. Contrary to what you might have been told or read about ghosts, they just as often appear in daytime. It might be because they have more energy than at night. I believe this to be true. When they want to frighten they choose the dark and it stands to reason to appear at the end of day when humans are tired, hungry and have evening duties and they are preparing for bed and relaxation. We are not dealing with good moods here.

Ghosts were thought to be loved ones and friends trying to get back to us and we have to drop that idea and realize these are evil spirits who are good at impersonating those who have passed on.

Actually, they have been quite remarkable at it because they're still convincing many today. To treat them for who they really are is what we are meant to do. When we take control then we will understand our advantages and appreciate our superior status. We are not only in control of our own lives, we're in control of theirs.

It will disappoint them and I guess they've wondered if and when we would ever catch on! We do not need to fear them. By our new actions they'll get the message.

Think of all the discoveries and great finds available to us if we weren't on that "treadmill, the daily hustle," "the ghost play!"

Granny O looked at Justi again and said, "Let's pull ourselves up by our boot straps and claim our rightful position in this life and free ourselves of the whirlwind and show the world that just because ghosts are mostly invisible we possess the power to spot them and we are aware of their hauntings and prove them unworthy of our attention and introduce them to exits of which they are now so familiar. Evil can only come in if we invite it. When we become one with our parents, "professors, teachers, priests, Rabbi's preachers, nurses, doctors, fire fighters, law enforcement, armed forces, monks, missionaries, reporters and news media and all who devote their lives to enlightening and publishing the truth we are destined to win. We are not occupying neutral territory. We are free and we intend to stay that way. With our praises, prayers, and worship of Almighty God we will send evil far from us. Our prayers of thanks are unending! Our coins are inscribed, In God We Trust," and so it is!"

Carvings

The view from atop a mountain range in autumn is beyond description. Sitting on this huge rock, scented breezes softly drifting by, wanting to believe that someone long ago passed this way and had the same thoughts I'm having now. From this lookout point there is not a trace so far of anyone having been here. There is still a visible trail due to the abundant wildlife. On the other side, the down trail being open, might expose some carvings, yet just take into account that those preceding me may have felt as I do and didn't want to spoil the beauty of the nature surrounding them. If so, silence is their spokesperson and nature their perfect teacher.

On the trail down, there are no traces visible. There is something here I'm missing. Nature knows something I don't know. What am I missing here? Thinking more deeply, I realize the answer is in the question I'm asking. Missing, it's me! I was missing and now I know. What isn't here is my answer. The lack of what isn't here is carvings. I was expecting a message, a clue and now I not only have my answer I also just inherited a clue as to what I'm supposed to do!

My own carving, how can that be? I only came by here and left, no time spent here to know what went on here, but I am expected to leave a trace of what has been! Again, I resort to quiet time, awaiting my informer's action to enlighten my thoughts.

I passed this way, inquisitive, wanting to know how it might have been. As I write, my pen leaving "traces in ink," resembling the impression made by the Egyptians in an artistic process in which a design is carved into the surface of a material, most often a sheet of copper. Ink was then applied. Paper or other absorbent material was laid on top of the plate. Applied pressure transferred the ink to the paper. "Intaglio" techniques have been used on coins, seals, medals and stone scarabs (charms) since 1200 BC.

In a curious way, I am carving the things that have passed my way and impressed and influenced my way of thinking so others can relate to how it was for my having been here.

My journey is not over. If I hurry, I can still be home in time for dinner! Yes and wonder and dream some more!

CHAPTER 7

Justi sat thinking for the next few minutes. She'd had quite an adventure finding Granny O's journal. She didn't understand it all yet, even though she and Granny O had just read through the whole thing. There were many questions going through her mind. She needed some time to think. One thing was clear. Granny O was putting forth the theory (or was it a hypothesis?) that there are evil spirits among us. They might be called ghosts but they are not the spirits of humans who have passed on. They are evil and they mean us harm. Thus, the word, Granny O, as a little girl coined "evolution" the way the evil spirits grow and work amongst us. She says we have the power to order them out of our homes and out of our lives or the power to invite them in. Wow! That's a lot of power!

Justi decided she was going to need a lot more visits and a lot more conversation with Granny O to sort this whole thing out.
Granny O interrupted her thoughts and asked if she had questions. Justi replied that she did but she wanted to think a while first. She hoped they could get together many more times before the summer was over. So, she and Granny O made a date to meet the following week. Justi would start her list of questions soon. She was instructed that for now, this was to remain their secret. And so it was.

ABOUT THE AUTHOR

I Conroy comes from a long line of Irish storytellers and continues the tradition. She has been telling stories, especially stories to children and about children her whole life.

Finally, at age 89, she began to write some of her many stories down. This story represents her first published work but there are many others written that are soon to be published.

.

www.ingramcontent.com/pod-product-compliance
Lightning Source LLC
Chambersburg PA
CBHW070646130626
46555CB00006B/2736